# A NOTE TO F

Congratulations on choosing the best in educational materials for your child. By selecting top-quality McGraw-Hill products, you can be assured that the concepts used in our books will reinforce and enhance the skills that are being taught in classrooms nationwide.

And what better way to get young readers excited than with Mercer Mayer's Little Critter, a character loved by children everywhere? Our First Readers offer simple and engaging stories about Little Critter that children can read on their own. Each level incorporates reading skills, colorful illustrations, and challenging activities.

**Level 1** – The stories are simple and use repetitive language. Illustrations are highly supportive.
**Level 2** - The stories begin to grow in complexity. Language is still repetitive, but it is mixed with more challenging vocabulary.
**Level 3** - The stories are more complex. Sentences are longer and more varied.

To help your child make the most of this book, look at the first few pictures in the story and discuss what is happening. Ask your child to predict where the story is going. Then, once your child has read the story, have him or her review the word list and do the activities. This will reinforce vocabulary words from the story and build reading comprehension.

You are your child's first and most influential teacher. No one knows your child the way you do. Tailor your time together to reinforce a newly acquired skill or to overcome a temporary stumbling block. Praise your child's progress and ideas, take delight in his or her imagination, and most of all, enjoy your time together!

Library of Congress Cataloging-in-Publication Data

Mayer, Mercer, 1943-
    Field Day / by Mercer Mayer.
        p. cm. – (First readers, skills and practice)
    Summary: Although Little Critter does not win any games at field day at school, his friends cheer for
him anyway. Includes activities.
    ISBN 1-57768-813-9
        [1. Racing—Fiction. 2. Schools—Fiction.] I. Title. II. Series.

PZ7.M462 Fi 2001
[E]—dc21                                                                2001026599

## McGraw-Hill
## Children's Publishing

A Division of The McGraw·Hill Companies

Send all inquiries to:
McGraw-Hill Children's Publishing
8787 Orion Place
Columbus, OH 43240-4027

Printed in the United States of America.

1-57768-813-9

1 2 3 4 5 6 7 8 9 10 PHXBK 06 05 04 03 02 01

 A Big Tuna Trading Company, LLC/J. R. Sansevere Book

FIRST READERS

Level 2    Grades K - 1

# FIELD DAY

by Mercer Mayer

McGraw-Hill
Children's Publishing

Columbus, Ohio

At school, we had a field day.
Miss Kitty took our class outside.
We played games.
We ran races.

4

5

Gator won the sack race.
We all cheered for him.

Tiger and Malcolm won the
wheelbarrow race.

We all cheered for them.

9

Gabby won the potato race.
We all cheered for her.

11

Maurice and Molly won
the three-legged race.
We all cheered for them.

13

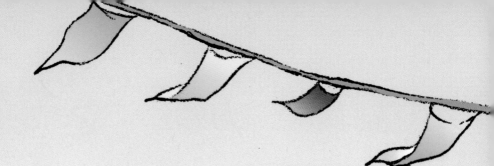

I wanted to win the egg race.
I tried my very best,
but my egg fell off the spoon.

15

It didn't matter about my egg.
My friends cheered for me anyway!

# Word Lists

Read each word in the lists below. Then, find each word in the story. Now, make up a new sentence using the word. Say your sentence out loud.

| Words I Know | Challenge Words |
|---|---|
| school | field |
| games | wheelbarrow |
| sack | cheered |
| potato | three-legged |
| egg | friends |
| spoon | |

# Who Won?

Match the question to the picture. Try not to look back at the story. The first one has been done for you.

Who won the
three-legged race?

Tiger        Malcolm

Who won the
wheelbarrow race?

Maurice      Molly

Who won the
sack race?

Gabby

Who won the
potato race?

Gator

19

# Name-Writing Practice

When you write your name, start with a capital letter. Then, write the rest of your name in lowercase letters.

Example: Gator

Gator

Practice writing your name on the lines below.

Now, practice writing names from the story.

Tiger

Malcolm

Gabby

Maurice

Molly

# Pronouns

Pronouns take the place of nouns. They include: I, he, she, it, they, you, and we.

Example:
Little Critter went on a field day.
He went on a field day.

He can take the place of Little Critter. He is a pronoun. Little Critter is a noun.

Match the picture to the pronoun.

he

she

it

they

22

# Give a Cheer!

Circle the pictures below that start with the same sound as the ch in cheer.